About the Author

After publishing his first book at the age of eleven, Raahem has been working hard in school as well as working on other novels. His first book *You Never See Me Coming*, which was greatly enjoyed by the general public, has become a great success in his home city of Ottawa. Raahem has been working hard on new novels and is happy to present another exciting story, *Welcome To The Good Hackers*. Raahem is excited to release new books and hopes that his book will be enjoyed by people of all ages.

Welcome to the Good Hackers

Raahem Syed

Welcome to the Good Hackers

Olympia Publishers
London

www.olympiapublishers.com
OLYMPIA PAPERBACK EDITION

A CIP catalogue record for this title is available from the British Library.

ISBN: 978-1-78830-684-3

First Published in 2021

Olympia Publishers
Tallis House
2 Tallis Street
London
EC4Y 0AB

Printed in Great Britain

Dedication

This book is for my parents, Moiz and Fauzia Syed, who have supported me through every endeavour I have ever experienced. You have done so much for me; I would be so lost without you. You have helped me with everything whenever I have needed it. What would people do without their parents? This book is also for my loving grandparents who have always been a great inspiration to me.

Prologue

James Miller. Position: White Hat Colonel

I will be telling you a story. A story that changed the world. A story that no one knows the complete truth about, except those who were there from the start. There were seven there that day. The day that marked a war. A war of technology. A war that makes people afraid to go on the most open, yet most referred to, database worldwide… the internet. This well-known danger to the world today possesses multiple threats to the world as we know it; downloadable products and differing forums have forced people into hiding as these modern-day Nazis have taken over their lives. I will tell you the tale of how all this began. I know that story. I was there when it all started. I was there for it all, and now I can tell the truth about what happened. What has happened since September, 2004. Because I was there, I was there when Adam Brown told us, “Welcome to the good hackers.”

These notes have been extracted from the journals and logs of the following seven:

Adam Brown, Ryan Hall, Melissa Taylor, Chloe Chapman, Cameron Gilbert, Daniel Wang, James Miller.

Nothing said or done in this book reflects on my personal character whatsoever.

– Raahem Syed

Chapter 1

Adam Brown. Position: White Hat General
Monday August 30, 2004

As I walked along the crowded street the sun was shining down, making elongated shadows over the grey pavement in Columbus, Ohio. The pleasant mood felt infectious, but I could not let that distract me. I had other things to worry about. I knew I had forgotten something, but I could not remember. While I was in my reverie a soccer ball came rolling towards me with an odd arrangement of colours, neon yellow with a bright neon pink. A young boy, around seven years old came running up to me. "Can I please have the ball, Mister?"

I regarded the boy. Surely, I was not someone who was old enough to be called Mister; alas, in the eyes of this little boy, anybody would be old enough. "Of course, here you go," and I passed him the ball. It rolled to him and lay at his feet. He scooped it up and ran to who I am assuming was his mother. Being a twenty-one-year-old, I must look like a giant to a boy that young. Then it hit me: Jackson Rodriguez was coming to my house at 4:00. If I ran at a steady speed of three miles per hour, I could reach my house in seven minutes. Jackson is my best friend. We have always been coding and white hat hacking. I taught him everything I knew three years back, and since then I have been writing computer programs with him. He had previously been charged with aggravated assault and is extremely impatient. He didn't get in much trouble, though, his dad being a very influential person. I started sprinting as fast as I could, doing calculations in my head to see if I could find a short cut. I could try to run across the football field but the chances of me getting chased and tackled depended on the athlete's speed, possibility of which was 78.8%. The biggest problem being that on average it would take nine minutes to start up my computer completely, and if I was late, then the computer would not start in time for Jackson to arrive. When I got home, I saw that Jackson hadn't arrived, even though I was late. I went in, said hi to my mom who was visiting me (it was her last day in town), and went upstairs to see if Jackson was already there. He wasn't, so I called him. "Hi Jackson, you coming today"? I asked him.

"Nah, can't today, sorry about that, Adam," he answered.

"Okay, see you when classes start up again," I tell him and end the call. I open my computer and I am greeted by my personal assistant, Amanda.

"Good afternoon, Adam. There are currently two malware encrypted codes being distributed at alarming speeds around you. Please enter your password to proceed," she says. I enter my password: M3e4l5i6s7s8a9. If you look closely and remove the numbers, the password is Melissa. Melissa Taylor is a girl I have had a crush on for a long time. She is super smart, she is also a computer programmer, a fine one. She can code and hack, and she is great, a great athlete, an all-in-one inclusive package. I look to see what hacks are happening. I had a hidden computer software running on the service provider's network but covering only the area across the city I live in for hacking detection. This is a time when breaching personal and/or organization security by hacking is a famous hobby among our university campus. For some it was just for fun, for some a challenge, and for the rest it was a means to make quick money either in the shape of ransom or by threatening to leak confidential information. The world was still trying to figure out how to deal with this new emerging technology. They were just starting to realize how to address the challenges faced by this completely new world, where anyone could pretend to be someone else or something else. New policies from the government must be put in place for this online world, new laws need to be created, new law enforcement units need to be established to address cyber challenges, but not yet. Right now, authorities' priorities are different from looking into cyber crimes and threats. Of course, some significant incident must happen before anyone starts looking into it seriously. Meanwhile I decided to use my capability to stop some of this craze, at least at a local level. My program (virus) on the network identified that one guy was trying to hack Amazon but failing, and there was someone else with a familiar coding sequence switching from C sharp to python with varying degrees of difficulty with layers upon layers of code, working away. Looking closely, I saw it was trying to hack my university's grading system. Whoever this was, was doing a great job of bypassing the fail-safe measures put in place by the security generation sequence. I focused in on that and tracked the IP address. When the search came back, it turned out to be Jackson's IP. What was he trying to do? Our deal was to always stay ethical. He looked to be accessing our class records. He was trying to alter a student's results. Shocked, I decided to go down to his house. When I got there his butler let me in. I walk up to his room and knock. He opens the door and is surprised to see me.

"Hello Adam, I didn't know you'd be coming down, what's up?" he asks.

"Nothing much, except for the fact that you are altering the university's results," I tell him.

"What's the big deal? It's not like that'll affect anyone, it'll only make Darren's life better," he tells me.

"This isn't why I taught you hacking!" I tell him.

"Nobody cares why you taught me hacking. Anybody ever tell you it's a free country? I will use this knowledge however I want," Jackson answers with agitation. He doesn't like the fact that I am trying to control or limit him.

I was furious to hear his response and I lose my cool. "You are nothing compared to me. Nothing. Your skills are satisfactory compared to mine. You will always be nothing. Always! There is nothing you can do that I can't stop!" I yell and start walking out.

"You just watch me!" he yelled back with rage.

Chapter 2

Adam Brown. Position: White Hat General
Wednesday September 29, 2004

It had been almost a month and Jackson and I didn't have any interaction with each other. Looked like he had closed all doors of communications. I know I had been a bit harsh with Jackson, and know for a fact that he is not at all happy with me. I have tried calling him, but he forwarded me to voicemail which he had changed to say, "If your name is Adam Brown never call me again" which really comes to show how petty people can be sometimes, especially when they are in the wrong. University started on September 7 and things were not the same. University was not the same.

After knowing what he was up to, I was also avoiding any interaction with him. You see, I had never told Jackson that I had a hack made especially for him, and I also didn't tell him that I have always had an eye on him and his tech (you wouldn't either). So, if he discovered that I am aware of his plans to start an organization, just to flood the internet with malware, as well as wreak havoc over the internet with his good-for-nothing friends

Darren Wilson, Janet Ross, Amy Simpson, and Jayden Brooks, his determination in proving he is better, and nobody can stop him, would only lead him to the point of no return. He called it Project Anonymous. His plans for September 30 went like this: he was gathering his associates right where we started our friendship, gym Resource Room #1 at 12:35 pm sharp as that is the time it is almost always abandoned.

Now, my own plan was to gather a team of like-minded people to be prepared for Jackson and his team's attacks. I always thought Jackson would be a part of my team; who knew I would be teaming up with others against him? He just has to be stopped. The name for my team is simple: "The Good Hackers". My team will comprise Melissa Taylor, Ryan Hall, Daniel Wang, Chloe Chapman, James Miller, and Cameron Gilbert should they choose to accept. Our meeting was scheduled for 12:40 in the Supply Room #4 which was also usually abandoned. I had already sent them an email and to my delight they had all responded with a yes; the email read thus, "I would like to invite you to discuss an important matter as I feel I can trust you as friends to help me in what I am looking to achieve. You all have been great friends to me, and I know I can discuss anything in confidence with you. If you accept this invitation, meet me tomorrow in the Supply Room #4.

What we will be going to be engaged in after tomorrow's meeting will be risky, but your character and skills reflect the reason you have been chosen. If you join, there is no turning back. However, I will do my best to make sure no one is harmed. Please do not share this email with anyone and I expect you to not discuss it at all, before we meet. I also expect you to delete this email after your response. Regards, Adam Brown" When I looked at my email, at first it looked scary and dangerous. However, everyone agreed, and I received a positive response within an hour from all of them, so I must have been overthinking. I then sent Jackson this message using the 64-bit coding algorithm I created, and Jackson had the decoder for this algorithm (which I had provided him while teaching/training him). "I know what you are planning, and I will stop it no matter what. Project Anonymous will never succeed," it read. I got an answer one minute later. "It already has," it declared with a picture of a vendetta mask beside it.

...

There were specific reasons to engage the people who were selected for the team, but what's common among all of them was that I was able to blindly trust them. I have known Melissa Taylor since middle school, and I have known that her technical skills were very strong. She and I used to compete in writing simulations for our school projects. She is 5 feet 6 inches tall and physically fit.

I met Chloe Chapman at a coding meet at the very start of freshman year and we bonded right away as her analytical skills and her programming style were very similar to mine.

Ryan Hall is one of my closest friends. Beside his technical skills I can count on his physical training and martial arts skills for any field work that may be required in future.

Daniel Wang is one of the smartest people I have ever met. I have known him since kindergarten. We studied together until grade five and then he switched schools to attend the gifted program, but we always maintained our friendship regardless of not seeing each other every day.

I got to know Cameron Gilbert through Ryan and our first meeting four years ago gave me a very warm feeling about him. He is the kind of guy who can make anyone comfortable around him. He is definitely a kind of a friend who will do anything for a friend. I always had great regard and respect for him. Cameron is physically very strong according to everyone who knows him. I needed someone who can be reliable in the field.

Chapter 3

Adam Brown Position: White Hat General
Thursday September 30, 2004, 12:40 pm

As everyone sat before me, I started talking. "Before I start sharing everything in detail with you, I would like to thank you for coming and attending this meeting. I know it was an ambiguous email I sent, but it was needed. All of you are good friends of mine and we have known each other forever. I know I can blindly trust you and your capabilities. I also know that you have a similar level of faith in me, and the fact that you are here, and a part of this meeting, clearly reflects what I just mentioned. I am also glad that every single one I approached showed up for this meeting, which is definitely encouraging for me (I say this with a huge and very relaxed smile on my face). Having said that, I would like to give everyone one more chance. If they do not want to be a part of this adventure, they can choose to leave now, and it will be completely understandable. I see that this is only going to be ugly and dangerous from here. If you are only staying due to the curiosity that has been built among all, I suggest as a good friend that you leave. As they say sometimes, ignorance is the blessing." I took a two-minute pause to let the people decide, and as expected no one left.

I started again with that same confident smile on my face, "OK. Well, as some of you already know, in the 1950s we were introduced to the first computers available to humans. Not long after we were introduced to hackers, but they were not started for a negative reason, they were *made* a negative reason. It wasn't until the 1980s that the term 'hacker' was used in a negative way, just because three people started something. Three people came to start something that now is difficult yet possible, and even harder to stop. Today we face an even bigger threat, a threat known as Project Anonymous." And then I tell them all of how I know about project Anonymous. "I know that right now at this very moment, Jackson Rodriguez is making his team of black hat hackers. You each have abilities that can be used to help people. Jackson chose the wrong path and I blame myself for that. I taught him almost everything he knows today about computer hacking. Today, I need you to stop him, though you cannot take credit for what you do as we have to be in the dark to protect the online society. Any questions?" I asked at the end of my short briefing.

Melissa raised her hand,

"Yes, Melissa?"

"Weren't you and Jackson Rodriguez best friends?"

"We were until I realized he was using his hacking for malicious things like changing university results," I responded with some pain in my voice. It definitely didn't feel the same without Jackson.

Cameron Gilbert then raised his hand.

"Why did you choose us?" I could see in his eyes that he wanted the assurance that I know what I am getting into and with the right resources.

"Because I saw something in you that I never saw in Jackson Rodriguez. You would not be here today if I had not been stupid enough to think that Jackson would always stay as a white hat hacker. That was a mistake on my part."

Daniel raised his hand.

"You know, I always support you and do not get me wrong, I am with you on this too, but why not inform the authorities? Why take such a big risk? We are not equipped with the right skill sets as we do not know what to expect forthcoming."

"Very good question, Daniel," I said with a calm voice. "I had thought the same, but with what evidence do I inform the authorities? I do not have any solid proof of their plan. Without any evidence, the authorities are not going to take any action. Besides, you all know that neither the authorities nor the law is equipped to address cyber attacks and crimes. On top of it, Jackson's father is a very influential person; no one will listen to us without any solid evidence. You are also right; we may not have all the required skill sets. I have a plan, though, and let me assure you that you will be the best after you have been trained, just for computers but to face other dangers too. We may have to infiltrate black hat facilities to stop what they are trying to do. I know Jackson very well. His ego is badly hurt, he will use all his father's resources and funds to build an organization large enough to hit around the world just to prove his point. One thing I know as of today is that Darren Wilson, Janet Ross, Amy Simpson, and Jayden Brooks have joined hands with Jackson Rodriguez, and they agreed to operate as black hat hackers."

"Hmm, makes sense, and I am with you as always," Daniel said with excitement.

"So am I," said Ryan. He and Daniel have been best friends and together since primary school.

"Seems like no more questions, no more confusion for people, which is a good thing," I said to myself with a faint smile.

To conclude the meeting, I continued, "Final words from me: Jackson and the team have decided to change their life. We will have to bring changes in our lives too. I am forming this team until the authorities and the law are ready to deal with cyber crimes. We may not only be up against these black hat hackers but many others; however, initially black hat hackers will be our focus while keeping a close eye on the others. You do not need to make this your day job, but you can not just take this out from your priority. I am glad that today I am surrounded by the right set of people who have integrity, character and passion to do something for the country and the world. I feel proud to tell you all today, Welcome to the Good Hackers." Everyone started clapping and I felt that my choice of people was a good one.

This was the start of something great, something that could and *would* change the world. They all looked at me expectantly. I answered the question I could see in all their eyes, "We start tomorrow after university. My shed is open for use." Everyone nodded. They all filed out of the room one by one, checking that the coast was clear. I knew that Jackson was meeting with his team in Resource Room#1. I decided to go with James Miller and Chloe Chapman just to remind him that I am not backing off. The pressure they would feel, especially when they see us outside their meeting room, might discourage them or cause a change of heart for some. We wait outside Resource Room #1 and two minutes later people start filing out in order: Darren Wilson, Janet Ross, Amy Simpson, and Jayden Brooks, and finally Jackson Rodriguez as expected.

"You better learn to mind your own business, Brown, or you might find yourself in trouble," Jackson said looking triumphant.

"You better learn that recruiting people to hack for you will come to a sticky end for all of you." His whole team stopped dead in their tracks.

"Nothing you can do about it, Brown," replied Amy Simpson.

"I am warning you, Jackson and you all, I showed my 'best friend' that I am ready to stop black hat hacking at any cost as Jackson probably told you. I can do this alone or with others; both ways I will win," I told them.

"You are here under false pretenses, Brown, you know nothing about what happened today in that meeting. Just mind your own business," Jackson told me with annoyance in his voice.

"I will say one last thing to you: I thought you would already know that I know more about you than you think, so watch your step," I calmly told him and then turned my back on him and walked away.

While everyone was leaving, I personally thanked Daniel and Cameron for joining the team; this work especially requires significant funding, and Daniel and Cameron can be a great help in this regard due to their families' financial background. They already have inheritance which I can describe as limitless; if they decide not to work at all and want to live a lavish life, and I mean lavish life, they can live in luxury for more than 1,000 years without any financial constraints. We will be needing funding in many areas, building HQ, having the right equipment to support our work, vehicles for transportation, transportation in general, etc. Daniel and Cameron being part of the team is one less stress on my shoulders: there is now no need to worry about funds to support the initiative.

Chapter 4

Ryan Hall Position: White Hat General
September 30, 2004, 2:50 pm

I didn't know why Adam Brown chose me of all people. I mean yeah, I might be OK in coding/programing but not as good as him or the others he chose for his team. It must be my fitness and the fact that I am a 3rd degree black belt in mixed martial arts. I'll tell you the truth; if I had not made the right choice today, I may have ended up in Jackson's team. I did receive a text from Jackson before I got one from Adam.

"If you are reading this, it means that you have been chosen to be part of something (big and interesting) due to your special abilities. It is dangerous. Peoples' perspective may be mixed about us, but I can assure you that you will have fun, you will feel the power and a new kind of control over the world and you will be able to live an upscale life. Just make sure that no one knows about this text and when I say no one, I mean no one! If anyone finds out about this text, there will be consequences." I said "No" right away, but after receiving Adam's text I was torn between what I wanted. I was confused initially when I received the texts from both of them. Are they (Jackson and Adam) talking about the same thing, being such good friends? But very quickly I realized by the tone of each text that they had each gone their separate paths.

I wanted to lead a normal life, I wanted to have a successful business in the medical field as I was studying to be a cardiothoracic surgeon. But at the same time, I have always wanted to do something good, make a difference, and I can get this opportunity by helping Adam Brown stop a worldwide cyber threat, which is going to be a very big threat very soon to every individual's life, groups of people and corporations. I decided to give it a try and as I typed "Yes", and wanted to click the send button, my finger hesitated. "Yeah, I may not be able to lead a normal life," I thought to myself and clicked send. Now, I am part of a team working to stop a threat involving hacking and physical training. Sure, I can do it.

I was raised with all the freedom. My parents let me do whatever I wanted to do with two limitations; not to lie, and always to share if anything significant is happening in life, making sure nobody is hurt by my actions. I remember very clearly, even when I was in kindergarten when my father came to pick me up, at the school gate, I could hear other parents asking their kids, "How was school?" or "Did you have fun at school?" or "Did you make new friends?" or "Did you learn anything new today?" But the first question my father always asked was, "So, did you help someone at school today?" This question made a great impact in my life and since childhood I have known that helping others is the way to livc.

I did not want to share this assignment I had accepted with my parents, I did not want them to be worried about anything. I had been trying to find a way to justify it to myself that task is not significant enough and doesn't need to be shared with them. Plus of course I will be helping so many people. Adam mentioned in the meeting that this shouldn't be your full-time occupation so merely doing it on a part-time basis, I guess that puts it in a non-significant category and I do not have to share it with them. I satisfied myself with that.

Daniel, Cameron, and Melissa arrived. "Hi guys, how's life?" I ask.

"Weird," replied Cameron.

"What? Do you want to be on Jackson's team? Or be completely left out! I am happy that someone is taking initiative," said Melissa.

"Quiet down, Darren is watching us," said Daniel quietly.

"Should we wait for James and Chloe, or take off?" I asked.

"Let's ditch, I want to get there early," replied Cameron.

"I'll stay behind," said Melissa.

Daniel, Cameron and I walked away towards Adam's house. "What are you hiding, Ryan?" Daniel asked me.

"Okay, I'll tell you. I got a message from Jackson as well. He asked me to join Project Anonymous. I said no. What about you?" I asked.

"I didn't," said Daniel.

"Neither did I," said Cameron. We continued walking towards Foxword Crescent where Adam's house was located. When we reached the house, he came out to meet us.

"Where are the others?" he asked.

"Melissa stayed back to come with Chloe, and James," Cameron explained.

"Dang, I hoped she was coming alone," he muttered.

"What was that?" I asked even though I already knew.

"Nothing," he said very fast. We waited in Adam's front yard, playing with Cameron's dog who was just visiting with Cameron's older brother. In ten minutes, we saw Melissa, Chloe, and James walking towards Adam's house. When they arrived, Adam led us towards his shed. As soon as we entered, we heard James say, "Hey!! We're working in this crap?" I looked around, calculations constantly running in my head.

"No, we aren't," Adam answered, "there is a trapdoor under the green bin." I gestured towards the small green bin in the corner of the shed questioningly. Adam walked over to the green bin wordlessly and grabbed the bin and moved it to the other side. He then opened the trapdoor and gestured for us to come down with him. We went down the ladder and Chloe closed the trapdoor behind herself. That's when it turned out that we were in an underground tunnel.

"Holy sh..."

"Language, James," I said as I interrupted him.

“We’re 21, Ryan, you and Daniel are the only university students who don’t swear,” James shot back at me.

“You want to hear me swear? ‘James Miller’,” I responded.

“Classic rebuttal,” Chloe chuckled.

“Not actually that classic, it’s quite new,” Daniel said.

“When me and Daniel are done with this, it’ll be heaven,” I told them.

“Well, this is where we will be working. Ryan and Daniel can renovate the HQ,” Adam said.

We all went out after Adam, everyone left in pairs, Melissa and Chloe, James and Cameron, Daniel and I. When we got to my house, I took Daniel upstairs to my room and took out my cell phone and put it down on my desk. “Okay! time to start designing our HQ,” I said.

Interruption

James Miller Position: White Hat Colonel

After that meeting, the next three months were very intense for all of us. There was a lot to do. Building a secure base, finding more trust worthy hackers, building identified skill sets, including physical training, keeping a close eye on Jackson and his team’s movements, arranging necessary equipment, transportation and much more. We were therefore unable to write logs and will be skipping straight from September to December.

Chapter 5

Ryan Hall. Position: White Hat General
December 12, 2004, 4:00 pm

We added our finishing touches yesterday to the "warehouse". Daniel and I invited the team to the warehouse for 4 pm so they must be on their way. I see them coming down the street together. They had previously been spying on Jackson's team. "Come on, guys, hurry up," I said. We walked into Adam's backyard. We entered the shed and went down the ladder.

"Wow! Welcome to paradise," James said sarcastically looking at the one rickety chair in the corner.

I went and slid over a panel in the metal wall. I entered in a passcode on the blue glass screen. The whole wall opened, and a voice said, "Welcome Ryan". "Wow" came from all around. Computers and comfy rolling chairs everywhere. It looked just like Tony Stark's basement from the Iron Man comics. The computer screens everywhere, control panels in front of the chairs.

"Welcome to HQ," said Daniel. "Good job, guys, let's get to work now." I went and sat down at the chair labeled Ryan Hall with a golden plate on the back. Everyone else went and found their chairs.

"Why is my name plate silver?" complained Cameron.

"Because you are a satisfactory member of the team," answered James.

"No, it's just because we didn't get the right order," I told Cameron. "Oh, and James, if the silver name plate means that you are a satisfactory member then what are you going to be?"

"What does that mean?" James questioned.

"Look closer at yours," I told him. James's looked at first sight gold, but it was actually bronze.

"You son of a b–" James started but then BEEP…BEEP…BEEP.

"What was that?" Adam asked.

"Oh, well, Ryan thought that since James swears a lot, we should add a system that every time James tries to swear in HQ there will be a huge beep. It's actually why it took us so long to finish, because I was programming the system," Daniel answered. "Hey, hey, hey guys, look – FBI International Chief Noah Moore is having a press conference."

Chloe pointed to the TV on the wall. "Melissa, can you please turn up the volume?" Chloe asked.

"Looks like the biggest challenge for FBI International to date," said Melissa after listening to part of the news.

Viewers, we just had a chat with the new Head of the FBI International, Noah Moore, who says that he will be the one to catch Bellator. We turn off the news and pretend like this doesn't concern us; well, it sort of does, but still.

"Wait, what did you guys manage to get when you were spying on Jackson's team?" I asked.

"We didn't exactly find anything that useful, we didn't find their headquarters. They didn't leave any trace about it, they are not even careless enough to accidentally leak any information. Oh yeah, and also they don't even talk to each other as far as we can see," Melissa finished.

"So technically we are clueless," James said, attempting to simplify things.

"Okay, guys, let's list down all of our skill sets, strengths and weaknesses to confirm working areas each of us should be focusing on," Adam said.

After the list was developed and work areas distributed, Chloe requested, "I am not sure about others, but I like to have a desk job. I love to work with decoding a 64-bit algorithm, Public vs. Private IP security, you know what I mean."

"I can do anything that is needed," Cameron answered.

"Same here," me and Daniel said at the exact same time.

"I'm extremely sorry that I have to say the same. I too agree with Cameron Gilbert," James replied sardonically. We all burst out laughing.

After few minutes of brainstorming and discussion based on everyone's expertise, it was summarized to be: James Miller, Ryan Hall, Daniel Wang, Cameron Gilbert, and Melissa Taylor set for field duty.

"So, I have a surprise for you all," Daniel said as he took out a box. "Here are some ear pieces for all of you so we can stay connected all the time."

"Thanks, Dan," I told him as I took one myself.

"Are these waterproof?" James asked.

"Yes," Melissa said from the side. "Don't you see how everything is covered up?" she finished as she put one on.

"What's the code?" called Cameron from the other side of the room.

"F12j04," Daniel answered.

"Is it possible to hack into the frequency that we use?" Chloe asked Daniel.

"Well, I can assure you one thing – that I secured the frequency with a code Jackson doesn't know of since I invented it, but other than that everything else is predictable."

"Wait, did you say that they don't seem to even talk to each other?" I asked Melissa. Oh yeah, I forgot to mention the fact that since Melissa and me have been in the same class since grade one we are really good friends.

"Well yeah, they just go about their business," she answers. "Oh, and yeah, they always keep their hood up on their way home," she added.

"I think they have got a frequency of their own," James said.

"It certainly seems like that, let's check it out," Daniel exclaimed, striding towards his chair. I went and sat down at mine.

"Oh yeah, I forgot to tell you my surprise. We've got around 800,000 people living here in Columbus, Ohio. I gave only 200 people the test to join The Good Hackers. They didn't know they were being tested for this, they thought it was just a survey. Thirty-seven people proved fit to be part of The Good Hackers, and they are now part of The Good Hackers. I will give you your positions, but for now we should thank Ryan and Daniel that they made this base able to accommodate a good number of hackers," Adam finished.

Adam was very clear about his role in all this. He decided to lead the base, especially when there are more good hackers expected to come and join. He knew that Jackson is just one threat when it comes to hacking; there may be many more out therc. Hc wanted to stop as many cyber threats as possible and one of the reasons for recruiting more hackers is to address this. It also makes sense for him to stay back in the base to provide the required support to The Good Hackers in coding and creating sophisticated programs to stop cyber attacks, as he is by far the best one among all of us.

Chapter 6

Melissa Taylor. Position: White Hat General
December 12, 2004, 4:45 pm

There are more members of the Good Hackers. I was already trying to process the fact that there are seven of us fighting crime, and now I have to work with another thirty-seven people. I find it too risky to have too many people, too many loose ends, but what Adam thinks is right and he has the final say.

"As we are going to grow soon, it is important to bring some structure to our organization. I am not here reinventing the wheel, and in my opinion, what is better than using the Security Forces' chain of command structure?" Adam said in one breath.

"Based on the many different criteria, I have ranked us all," he continued.

"Ryan Hall: Major General, Daniel Wang: Major General, Melissa Taylor: Brigadier General, Chloe Chapman: Colonel, Cameron Gilbert: Colonel, James Miller: Major."

"Why do I have such a low rank?" James complained.

"As I said, the ranks are given based on many considerations. When the time is right, you will be promoted," Adam answered.

"Wait, how did you know about Project Anonymous?" Daniel asked Adam. Personally, I don't care that much about how Adam knew about Project Anonymous, but that was my personal opinion.

"I have had all eyes on Jackson's devices," Adam answered.

"And you're sure of that," Ryan said, "since Jackson texted me as well to join Project Anonymous, and I know that Melissa was texted as well. I know the reason, but I'll keep it quiet for now," Ryan finishes. Yes, I had told him, in the eight years that we've known each other, we've learned to trust each other.

"Wait, what!" Adam said, his fingers surfing through the keyboard and typing characters into the computer.

"I know this is a bit off-topic, but I was just wondering when will the team of selected people be arriving?" Cameron asked.

"In two hours," Adam answered while still typing.

"Oh shi-" BEEP BEEP BEEP "I can't even access their systems, wait – I think I got it, James was talking to himself with beeping going off in the background

Then came the voice.

"Hello, this is Anonymous, knowing that you have accessed this server we will now take full control of every server belonging to you. Anonymous is coming for you. We Are Anonymous." I looked at it in shock. Whoever it was, was wearing a vendetta mask. I looked at Adam; he himself looked worried.

"We underestimated them," is all that Adam was able to say.

"Well that's that, why don't we figure out about their base so that we can stop them from taking control of the systems," Ryan said.

"How do we know there even is a base?" I asked.

"Isn't it obvious, the only thing that can take this down is a full lab," Ryan answered me.

"Okay, use the earpieces, James, Ryan, Melissa, and Daniel," Adam commanded.

"Don't you think we should brainstorm ideas about where the Anonymous base could be?" James asked.

"One of Jackson's dad's businesses is a construction company and their biggest accomplishment is…"

"Rodriguez Tower Luxury Apartments," Cameron finished the sentence for Daniel.

"Yes, it must be that. It is in a quiet area and Jackson always had a plan to use this building for his first business venture," Adam said in contemplation.

"Here's the plan! You four will be deployed in the Rodriguez Tower where you will be searching every area open to you and also those closed such as the Presidential Suite # 1, Jackson's room. Take a night gun, sixty-four bullets, and if you flick this button it turns to fifty-seven bullets of tranquilizers. One dart equals four hours of sleep." Adam finished flicking a button on the night gun. He passed one to me, James, and Daniel. He gave two to Ryan.

"Wait, how did you get hold of these?" I asked.

"My uncle ships weapons to the army. The army wanted this but then they cancelled the order. He was declaring bankruptcy. I saw the opportunity. The warehouse along with his business is ours, thanks to Cameron," Adam answered.

"I shouldn't have asked," I responded.

"You are the leader on this mission," he told Ryan. "Now, we just have to call in our extra team." He passed Ryan a backpack. "Here are some hacking supplies you probably know how to use." He then strode over to his computer and typed in some codes. "Okay, it will take them around five minutes to arrive, you four stay safe, you can go ahead; oh yes, Danicl, you arc Ryan's second – let's hope you don't have to take over." We left the base saying nothing, anyways what could have been said at that time, when there was a possibility that we could get hurt?

"Hey, are you guys here?" Cameron said into our earpieces.

"Yep," James said.

We got into the van and started driving to our first mission. To avoid suspicion, we parked our van a block away from the address. We continued walking towards Rodriguez Tower Apartments. When we finally got there, Ryan spoke.

"We have to split up. I'll search Jackson's suite. Daniel, search the whole lobby for floor plans. James, can you please search the floors for any secret entrances with Melissa, that'll go faster."

Chapter 7

Daniel Wang Position: White Hat General
December 12, 2004, 5:30 pm

I had the job of searching the lobby as Ryan had instructed. How would I explain to the security why I was searching through the building manager's floor plans? I had no idea. I think Ryan had the most dangerous job today. "Does everyone copy?" came Ryan's voice from the earpiece.

"No, we are all dead," James replied sarcastically.

I started moving around inspecting the doors and pretending to be lost. I then put my hand in my pocket to switch my night gun to tranquilizer mode. I don't want to kill anyone. I have never wanted to. None of us has ever wanted to kill anyone. It is not in us. We only want to help people.

"Okay, I'm outside Jackson's room right now," Ryan told us. "I need a status report right now from all of you."

"I'm trying to find the manager's office," I told Ryan.

"We are on the second floor searching," Melissa told Ryan.

Then I see what I was looking for, a door with "manager" written on it in gold. I walk over and knock. No answer. I walk in and see the empty chair. I shut the door behind me and take out my night gun. "Hey Ryan, I'm in the office."

"Okay Dan," came the reply.

"There is nothing in Jackson's room."

"Nothing on any of the floors either," James said. I walked over to one of the two filing cabinets and looked through the files but the floor plans weren't there. In the second one I found a smaller folder labeled "floor plans". Bingo. I opened it up, but instead of the blueprints there was just a picture of a vendetta mask, and the phrase "We are Anonymous". Then I heard a knock on the door. I slipped the folder into my jacket and hid behind the desk, my night gun in my hand. The door opened and Darren Wilson walked in.

"I know someone is here, reveal yourself," Darren said shutting the door behind him. I could see a knife in his hand. This was my only chance. I stood up and shot him squarely in the chest. He dropped like a marionette whose strings were cut loose.

"Hey Ryan, we have a situation here. Darren Wilson walked in and I shot him with a tranquilizer," I told him.

"Okay, find the files and we'll bring him with us," Ryan replied. I went on to the manager's computer and hacked it so I could access the files within. Of course, there must be a copy of the files on the computer in case it got misplaced. I found the floorplan files, but there was still only a vendetta mask and the words "We are Anonymous".

“Ryan, there are no plans, they have all been taken by Anonymous.”

“Okay, in that case I need you to somehow manage to get Darren to HQ. Wait, give me a second, Dan, I’ll ask Adam what to do,” Ryan said. “So, Adam says he is sending in reinforcements.”

“Umm. Okay. Let’s live with that,” I said. I waited there looking for clues.

“Hey, Daniel, it’s me, Adam. Reinforcements have just arrived. You cannot talk to them via communication device. I made sure that your frequency is not revealed to anyone. We just can’t take any risk. They are at the corner of the street. Let me know where exactly Darren is in the building and they will come get him from there.”

“Adam, please inform the reinforcements that Darren is on the ground floor, fifth door on the left after crossing the lobby. It has a Manager’s Office plate on the door.” I provided the details to Adam.

“Dan, leave the room. Reinforcement will be there shortly,” Adam suggested.

We continued our search for any clues for another ten minutes and then we heard James’s voice over the ear pieces, “So, guys, are we leaving? There’s nothing here.”

“Of course, there is something here, why the heck do you think Darren Wilson was here, if there is nothing here?” Ryan said angrily to James.

“So what? Are we going to check every piece of shit that goes down the toilets here to see where it goes?” James retaliated.

“What point are you trying to make? Of course not, if they don’t want to have crap falling in their base,” Melissa told him heatedly.

“Wait guys, I’m going to the main floor bathroom,” Ryan said.

Chapter 8

Ryan Hall. Position: White Hat General
December 12, 2004, 6:15 pm

Yes, after all that, one thing that I had deduced was that there was a high possibility that their base was in the least obvious place, in this case, a bathroom. I thought it to be a possibility since it is the place everyone visits the most, but I mean, I could always be wrong.

"You are what?" James yelled into the earpiece. "We are trying to find a hacker base and you… you… need to do a… a urine expulsion."

"No, you idiot, I am going to find their base, so please do me a solid and shut up," I answered angrily. I walked into the main floor bathroom, shut the door without locking it and inspected the room. It was a tiled wall with two feet by two feet tiles. I went and checked out the wall. The wall opposite the door was a regular wall. I knocked on it and it was solid. However, when I went to the wall opposite the sink and toilet, the grooves were clearly different and after knocking on the wall, I figured out that it was hollow. I opened the backpack that

Adam had given me, and I took out a crow bar and prised open the wall which turned out to be a door.

Right in front of the door was a metal door with an electronic keypad. “Hey guys, I found the door to the base. Adam, I am going to need a backup team of 15 people. I will also need you to send some of them with rifles for me and my team. Daniel, you wait for the backup team. James and Melissa, come to the main floor bathroom, start in three, two and one,” I finish.

“I am sending a team, led by Cameron. I’ll see you at the end of the mission,” Adam told me. I started to examine the key pad as Melissa and James walked in.

“Please tell me you’ve cracked the code,” James said, sounding bored. I didn’t answer him (knowing his attitude that was him getting started). I took out an infrared scanner and scanned the keypad. Though the heat signatures are minimal, I could still see signatures on 7, 6, and 3. The signatures on 7 were slightly more heated.

“Guys, the heat signatures are on 7, 6, and 3. They are slightly more visible on 7, what do you think?” I asked them

“Isn’t it obvious? The code is 7637,” James said almost immediately.

“No, it isn’t,” Melissa answered.

“And you call me stupid,” James said to himself more than anyone. “I’ll explain. On a phone, the letters are coordinated with the numbers, for example the number 2 is A, B, and C. On a phone the number 7 is R, 6 is O and 3 is D meaning the numbers mean RODR,” he finished.

"That makes sense, RODR from RODRiguez, thanks James, how did you know?" I asked him.

"Oh, you don't know how many times I call my girlfriend, Katie, you know. Actually I'm surprised she hasn't called yet," James finishes. I pressed in slowly 7-6-3-7. The door opened. Now, we had to wait for the reinforcements.

And after about twenty minutes seventeen people walked in. Daniel and Cameron were in the lead.

"Perfect," said Melissa.

"Let's go. Here, pass me a rifle," I said. One of the "soldiers" handed me a rifle and I walked in through the metal door down a staircase while switching my rifle to tranquilizer. "Come on now, slowly, we have to stay quiet," I whispered to the team. There could be no mistakes made. Then we saw the end of the staircase and we ducked into the shadows. There were approximately seventy unarmed people sitting at computers in this room. "Everyone switch to tranquilizer and take aim at the two people nearest the emergency buttons and the security cameras. I can see an Anonymous folder a few feet away. Take aim, on my signal," I told the team. Everyone chooses someone to shoot, and then "Fire" I whispered, and the tranquilizer darts flew through the room making no noise and hitting the targets. We all pulled on black masks and ran out of hiding. I switched to real bullets to create a diversion and I shot the ceiling. I already knew that this was a battle won for The Good Hackers.

Chapter 9

Melissa Taylor Position: White Hat General
December 12, 2004, 7:30 pm

We all rushed in. Ryan shot the ceiling with a few real bullets and after a few screams, he had everyone's attention. "We are The Good Hackers. This is a hostage situation. Stop everything you are doing at once and gather in the center of the room. All resistance will be met with force." He motioned towards the team and all of us holding either pistols or rifles. The group included Amy Simpson and Jayden Brooks. Everyone piled to the middle; some of them sat down. Each of them was shocked. "What you are doing is illegal. Black hat hacking is illegal as you all should surely have known. If it wasn't a police raid, then it is The Good Hackers who take it to a hostage situation." He finished. He motioned for Daniel and me to go and upload all their status onto our hard drives.

"This is Adam Brown's team. These are the heroes of earth". Said Jayden Brooks in a sarcastic manner. "Let me tell you, Hall, you and your team are nothing but shit," Jayden Brooks said. Ryan did not retaliate but James stepped forward and kicked him in the stomach. Jayden fell to his knees and before he could get up, James started for another kick in the face this time.

"JAMES!" Ryan exclaimed. "Stop, we are not here to terrorize people. It's in and out remember that."

James paused, then said, "That was an example of what would happen to anyone who thinks they have the right to blab, so let's keep from me getting you to vomit shit," James finished.

Meanwhile Daniel and I were taking all the information off the computers, even if most of it was encoded. We could decode it at HQ. Then Ryan whispered in James's ear (I could hear because of the ear pieces),

"We need to figure out where Jackson is. Can you do the honours?" he said.

"No prob," James answered. He walked over to the still winded Jayden and grabbed him by his collar and lifted him up.

"Where is Rodriguez? Tell me or it's a kick up your ass."

"He's not coming today," Jayden croaked.

"Why, you idiot? Why isn't he coming?"

"He left earlier today, around an hour and a half ago." James flung him to the floor and returned to Ryan. Amy Simpson hurried over to make sure that Jayden was okay.

"What now?" James asked.

"It depends. Melissa, Daniel, you two done there?" Ryan asked us through the earpieces.

"Just a minute for both of us," Daniel answered glancing at my screen.

"Who have they hacked?" James asked lamely.

"Mostly all the WiMAX towers in from Columbus up to New York. If you look at the WiMAX coverage right now on these, you can see that every 30-40 miles only one tower is working and even then it is not providing coverage to its full extent," Daniel finished.

"Okay, we're done," I said.

"And we are leaving," James said, and we all headed towards the exit.

"You will pay for this," Amy Simpson said to our backs.

"Wait, are you talking literally like you will hack our bank accounts or something?" James said sarcastically

"Come on," Ryan said, and we hurried out.

...

When we arrived back at HQ, we were greeted by a huge crowd. As soon as we got in, we saw a bunch of people waiting there chatting happily. When we arrived, everyone from the original crew came over and greeted us, and Chloe gave me a quick hug. We walked over to Adam, who smiled at me. Daniel and I took out our hard drives and gave them to Adam. "They contain everything Anonymous has hacked, planned to hack, and more," Daniel told him.

"This is great," Adam told him.

"I'm going home, Adam. Nice helping you out, call me if you need me," Ryan told Adam and before anyone could stop him, he walked right out of the base.

"So, what about Darren Wilson?" I asked Adam.

"And what to do with him," James came over to talk.

"Well he'll wake up in around two hours and then we can question him, good cop, bad cop style and try to get as much information as possible before we let him go."

"Okay, can I leave early then?" I asked Adam.

"Yeah, Ryan is gone anyways so–" Adam got cut off by the HQ telephone.

"Yeah, hi guys, it's me, Ryan. There were four people waiting outside my house. I was hoping maintenance could come and pick up the unconscious figures lying on my lawn. I think that two of them might be bleeding," Ryan says over the speaker.

"Okay, Ryan, I'm sending a team now," Adam answered and assembled the team to be sent to Ryan's.

"Oh, yeah, and I was wondering why there were 50 or so people in Jackson's base?" Ryan asked.

"As long as you scanned the room, I'll find out by tomorrow," Adam told him.

"Okay then, bye." And the call ended.

"So, who's up for working from home?" Adam asked as he dialed Ryan's number again on the phone.

Chapter 10

Chloe Chapman. Position: White Hat Brigadier General
December 12, 2004, 10:05 pm

I had volunteered for the night shift as Adam had asked everyone to take turns. Ryan had said that he would be active when he was sent any information. We had to report to him now. He was our team leader for field operations. I kept walking home until I heard a rustling sound behind me. Then four people jumped out of the bush behind me. Two grabbed my arms while two came in front of me and started hitting me repeatedly. "Keep hitting her. Don't stop until she's almost dead," said a voice in front of me that I recognized immediately. Janet Ross. Just then I heard a voice behind me. Everyone froze.

"The only person who should be beaten up that badly is you, you piece of crap," Adam said.

"I thought you told them to keep hitting. T =hey seem to have stopped," Cameron inquired.

"I am surprised you didn't bring along Hall to do the dirty work," Janet said.

“No, he has better things to do, but if you were wondering where Darren was, tell Jackson that The Good Hackers have him,” Adam said. Then Adam signaled Cameron and they both charged towards the Anonymous team who were all wearing masks. I caught a bunch of mixed up words including the F-Word which I do not write on logs. After that there was a huge pile of trash on the floor (I mean the Anonymous team), so Adam and Cameron left to call in the garbage truck to clean it up. I walked to my house, unperturbed that I had just been attacked by fellow classmates, unlocked the front door, said hello to my parents who were watching TV, went into my bedroom and opened my laptop. I accessed The Good Hackers secure network which was used in HQ as well and got to work finding footage from the Anonymous base. I needed to scan all the faces in that base to figure out who they were and then maybe we could put a stop to it. I found the footage easily and scanned every face there. It took a while because I had to use my computer to draw out where every face was. I then clicked save and send results and a loading bar appeared on my screen. Then in about 30 seconds, it showed my email and I clicked <<To Ryan Hall>>, <<CC: Daniel Wang, Adam Brown>> and sent them all the face scans. I also added a note for Ryan saying <<Most of the faces look familiar, check it out.>> I hit send and got a reply from Ryan almost immediately <<Good work Chloe, I’ll check out your concerns. You are relieved of duty until further notice. P.S. Adam has a surprise for us tomorrow at the Alum Creek Lake. He’ll give you the timing tomorrow. See you there.>> I then saw that I had an email from Adam. <<Here are the names of the new recruits: Maria Hernandez, Katie Garcia, David Smith, James Johnson…>> The list kept going. I closed my email and looked for myself which names had turned up, not thinking much of it until two names caught my eye, Maria Hernandez and Katie Garcia. I stared in shock at the names. I opened my email to check that those were the names and sure enough they were. I picked up the landline phone on my desk and called HQ. A woman's voice came out, "Thank you for calling the WiMax Plus accounts. Please enter your password." I hurried and dialed 1206 and was immediately transferred to HQ.

"Hi there, Chloe," James's voice sounded through the phone.

"Quick, give the phone to Adam," I said frantically.

"Sure, what's the hurry?" he asked.

"QUICK!" I yelled.

"Hello Chloe, what's wrong?" Adam asked.

"Where were Maria Hernandez and Katie Garcia during our mission?" I asked him.

"Katie was here at HQ, and Maria was with the team," Adam answered.

"Well according to the footage, they and multiple other Good Hackers' new recruits were at the Anonymous base at the same time," I told him.

"Wait, let me check," he said, "what the heck?"

Chapter 11

Adam Brown Position: White Hat General
December 13, 2004, 00:45am

Here's how it went, all in a flash.

"Well, according to the footage, they and multiple other Good Hackers' new recruits were at the Anonymous base at the same time," Chloe told me.

"Wait, let me check." I checked the footage for myself and checked the names. Then it dawned on me. "What the heck?"

"Thanks Chloe, you've been a big help," I told her and closed the phone. Then the telephone rang again.

"Hello Adam, it's me, Ryan, we've been duped by Anonymous," he said.

"I already know," I answered. "They beat us this time. I will–" I wasn't able to complete my sentence as I was interrupted by Ryan.

"Don't get too frustrated, Adam, this will all work out. What I am confused about is how Anonymous found out that Maria Hernandez and Katie Garcia are on our team. You saw the other names; all of them work for us."

"I know," I sighed and then continued. "It's just that you know as well as I do that this is all my fault. I put too much faith in Jackson, and this is the reason that all of this is even happening."

"Adam, you have to understand that none of this is your fault. None of us could have predicted this is how Jackson would have reacted. There is a way, though," he answered.

"How?" I asked.

"You know that it is easier to black hat hack than it is to white hat hack. Well, with black hat hacking there is less insurance that it will go unnoticed and it is definitely not irreversible. If we can look at the footage again–"

"But that is the footage we stole from Anonymous, so how can we just change it?" I cut in.

"I was getting to that. If we hack into their systems, we may be able to reverse everything using their systems," he told me. "There is one more thing. Not everything written in Melissa's log is accurate. We did take all their files on their employees; none of them were electronic but they were all put in file folders. While James created a diversion, Melissa and Daniel did not just download all the electronic information, they also took everything in paper," Ryan answered.

"Whose plan was this?" I asked, trying not to sound too happy.

"Cameron's idea," Ryan told me.

"Okay, I'll thank him tomorrow, but today, I need those files. Who has them?"

"They are at HQ. I put them on my desk before I left," he told me.

"Okay, bye then. Thanks for all the help. Next we have to take down all the Anonymous members one by one."

"Let's leave it at figuring out who they are and how they know who's on our team. One more thing. Send out a warning to all the Good Hackers. They are all in danger now that they know we have Darren, speaking of which he needs to be dropped off at home by 10:00. Bye," he says and ends the call. I go to his desk and see the file folders. There are around sixteen to seventeen file folders which are overflowing with papers. I grab three that are labeled "TEAM". The first ones are of course Darren Wilson, Janet Ross, Amy Simpson, and Jayden Brooks. Then there are some familiar and some unfamiliar faces. The biggest mistake Anonymous has made is too have added every piece of information they have on their employee – for example, Jayden Brooks, Address: 2453 Penny Street. Full name: Jayden Carter Brooks, blah blah blah. It just gives us more of an advantage. I keep looking through the files until I find a name that is all too familiar. Mia Brown. My cousin. I pick up my cell phone and dial her number.

"Hello Adam, what's up?" I hear her voice on the phone.

"Hello Mia, where have you been lately, I don't see you around much?" I ask her.

"Well, you know, I'm just around, you know," she tells me.

"How have you been using that hacking I taught you?" I ask her sternly.

"Why do you ask?"

"There have been rumors going around that there is a black hat hacking organization in town," I tell her.

"There have been rumors going around town that there is a *white* hat hacking organization in town." That confirms my belief. She is a part of Anonymous.

"Look Mia, I know that you are part of the organization that call themselves Anonymous. You may be my cousin, but I have no problem bringing you down. I will expose you for the fraud you are, to your parents, and everyone else you love. This is a warning: what is about to go down is going to be the downfall of Anonymous. Tell Darren, Jayden, Jackson, whoever you want. None of them can predict what will happen to you all. No one knows what we will do but it will destroy you all, just like no one knows where Bellator will go next." I end the call. "Maria, call the Generals, it's time we start Operation Downfall."

Chapter 12

Daniel Wang Position: White Hat General
December 13, 2004, 11:45pm

Our confidence seems to have greatly grown in the past few hours; one minute we were so nervous to pull off one simple break in {New note: August 14, 2011 <<Looking back I think pulling off a break-in should have been nerve wracking. Maybe I was just trying to act braver than I was, calling it simple, still who knows>> End Of New Note} and then the next we were starting Operation Downfall which was at that moment strictly forbidden to be written down in logs, for if Anonymous got hold of them, then our plan would most certainly be doomed. Still, when I got the call from Maria Hernandez, saying that tomorrow we would be discussing Operation Downfall, I must say I was a bit surprised. On our first day we had done a break-in, stolen all their information and files and had pulled off a hostage situation with James's help. Still, we will have to wait for tomorrow to see what happens.

...

December 13, 2004, 3:45pm

I arrived at the Good Hackers' base around 3:45 pm the next day. Everyone was already there waiting for me. I quickly apologized for being late and headed down into the base. The Generals headed into the meeting area. We all sat down, everyone except Adam who remained standing. "We have now officially commenced Operation Downfall. First off you can now start to add Operation Downfall on your logs as they seem very incomplete without any mentions and it removes the proof of concept that you guys have been in multiple meetings and not written anything down about it." It is a good thing that we got that sorted out, I think to myself. "Operation Downfall will expose all the hackers that are a part of Anonymous before they do anything that will cause lasting harm to the internet world. Remember, not all of their intentions may be bad, but we must take into consideration the fact that they are a group of black hat hackers and they will still attempt to hack our government, our banks, and our lifestyles. It started with WiMAX; next thing you know we will have no control over our phones and our computers. If we do not stop them now, we will be responsible for when they take over the world. We will bring them down, make it impossible for there to be an organization called Anonymous. Anonymous will never die, as long as there are people to continue its legacy. Now I should inform you about what happened last night at our HQ. We did, before sending Darren home, question him. These were his words before we put him in the car to take him home. He seemed to be switching between reality and hallucination at the same time. It felt hopeless after a few hours. He had, to use the common phrase, 'gone psycho'. He was biting the bars of his cell and scratching the walls while hurting himself as well. We dropped him off but stayed outside to see if Jackson or someone would come for him, but a few minutes later his dad dragged him out and put him in the car. Now he is at the hospital although no one knows how he got there. He was transferred to Ohio State University East where he is being held in the psychiatric ward, and kept under the pretense of minor trauma. We believed this may have been his plot for escape. He may even as we speak be devising a way to escape his ward. Our next mission was to get him out of there before Jackson could get his hands on him, and the effects of the tranquilizer wore off. We still had a lot of questions for him. Keeping him at HQ wasn't safe; it was better to let him off and get hold of him later. Your mission is to enter the hospital and change up their documents on this unknown patient. Give him an alias and write out a whole file for him, give him a major seizure problem or something."

"Couldn't we just change the files electronically?" James asked.

"Not all hospitals have adopted the new technology of keeping everything on their computer systems. They do print out the files, and every patient is kept on the patient registry, which has an electronic file and a hard copy. You can change the specific page for Darren on the online registry and switch the specific page in the registry. Make it that patient unknown has been released, and that a new patient by the name of say, ummm, Liam Jones. Does everyone understand?" Adam asks.

"Yes," everyone said in unison.

"Well then, get moving, chop, chop, it's only a matter of time until Anonymous finds out that Darren is being held there and even less until he escapes. I want the whole operation planned out by 7:30 this evening. Ryan, I want you to determine everyone's exact position and at which time tomorrow; I have the blueprints right here. Daniel, I need you to write out the fake file for the hospital with Cameron. Chloe, I need you to get access to the hospital registry. James, can help you with that. Melissa, I need you to get each of us except me an alias to get into the hospital; we need a reason to be there. As I said before, I need the mission layout by 7:30 tonight," Adam finishes, "Melissa, I am going to need you to work with me so that every alias is coordinated with everyone's positions. We need everything to be exact if we want this to work out," Ryan tells Melissa.

Chapter 13

Ryan Hall. Position: White Hat General
December 13, 2004, 5:00pm

"Okay everyone, get moving," I said. "We need to get this done as fast as possible. We cannot let Darren escape or worse, let Anonymous get to him." I sat down at my desk and invited Melissa over. "Melissa, here's what I am going to need from you: make realistic aliases, give us each a job as like a temporary nurse or something, do not make any of us a surgical resident! We'll kill people. But just sit down here, tell me your ideas, and we'll work from there," I told her.

"Okay, how's the name John Smith?" she asked.

"Why?" I answered.

"Your alias, genius," she said to me, sarcastically.

"Okay, yeah , that works," I told her, feeling stupid. "Melissa, I need to tell you something," I told her.

"What is it?" she asked.

"Uhhh, it's about Adam. He uhh…"

"How is the work here going?" Adam cut in.

"Good, I just finished Ryan's alias," she answered. Adam walked away as I started reading over my alias, Ryan Hall aka John Smith, Temporary Manager.

"What happened to the real manager?" I asked her.

She walked to her desk and then same back with a pill. "Injected with influenza," she told me proudly.

"Where did you get it?" I asked her.

"The other genius made it," she told me, looking over at Cameron.

"What do you mean the other genius, what did Cameron make for you?" I asked her.

"Oh, he makes me things all the time, computers, stuff likc that, every time I ask."

"Yeah I know that, but you've never called him a genius," I told her. "Anyways, what did Jackson give you as a gift?" I asked her.

"Ryan, shut the hell up," she told me.

"So, you still think he is a saint?" I asked her.

"Ryan, that's enough," she told me.

"You know out of everyone you could have chosen it had to be Jackson. There are other people," I told her. "And anyways, once it's out people will start thinking you are a spy."

"Who else is out there? Adam will never like me, he's always cold shouldering me. You, Dan, and Cam aren't into anyone and James is already with someone."

"Just think about it, and remember he is EVIL," I told her and got back to work.

...

December 13, 2004, 7:25pm

"Okay, it's all set," Chloe told me, "everything is done."

"Perfect, I've checked that everything is perfectly coordinated," Cameron answered.

"Let's head on to the meeting room," I told them. We all walked into the meeting room, where Adam was sitting in the head's chair; he was holding his head like he was having a severe migraine. He looked up as we entered.

"Is it done?" he asked; an expression of hopefulness lights up his face as he asked.

"Yes, we are done," Cameron told him.

"I'm sure any of us could have told him, Gilbert," James said coldly.

"Your mood has been shit lately, why?" Melissa asked James. "We will have plenty of time to discuss that later. Ryan, please start."

"Okay here is the plan. Cameron Gilbert will be posing as James Carter, temporar–"

"Why does he get the name James?" James whines.

"Because this is an alias, you dimwit," Chloe told him.

"Anyways," I continued, "he will be posing as James Carter, temporary case manager where he will be able to access the electronic files and change up the electronic files on Darren. It's pretty easy, but the hard part is when we'll go on a mission today and slip an influenza pill into the real manager's water or something that he is cooking.

That's Cameron's job. James will be going into the hospital as the new Human Resources and Recruiting Agent. His name will be Christian Brown. He will, however, cause some havoc and storm out by resigning on the spot once his job is over. Hopefully he won't attract much attention for too long. He will be working to interview all the main desk secretaries. That's where Chloe comes in; she will be posing as a secretary where she will put the fake registry page in the registry so that everything is clean. James will interview the secretaries since there is more than one and they will notice if she switches anything. Her cover is that she works the night shifts. Chloe will then trigger an alarm stating that patient Liam Jones, who was registered yesterday under 'mentally confused', and with a personality disorder, has left his secure ward, number 4357, which is currently available as a private ward. She will be going in as Allison Gray. Daniel will go in as a medical assistant and will have Darren transported from his current location to the ward. Daniel will trigger something in Darren's memory as Daniel was the one who shot him. He will suggest to the doctor to inject him with sleeping medication. When he is under the influence of such drugs, Daniel will inject him with a non-metallic tracker, which can be used to track Darren's location. Daniel will also put a tracker on his wristband. Melissa will be on hand to control any situation that starts to go out of hand; she will be present during the transfer of Darren so that if needed she can shoot him with a blow dart from a safe distance. Anyways, I'll be outside in the truck controlling the whole situation. You each will have either a watch, a necklace, or a ring with a tracker on it so I know everyone's position. Remember, you must keep in touch; this way I will inform you on what to do. Everyone must carry a gun in their back pocket at all times. Now, Cameron, you will be using this USB to change the online files up. Remember to do this in stealth because people will be able to see if you make changes on the regular one. James, you will get this list of the secretaries coming in tomorrow as well as this list of questions to ask them. Chloe, you will be getting the registry page, and the alarm you will ring is a red button underneath your desk, then pick up the intercom and inform the hospital. Melissa, you will have a blow dart and a gun in your back pocket. In case of an emergency, either one of you can say the phrase 'we have a problem' and I will get the building under lockdown. I will come in before this happens, though. If you are discovered, say the phrase 'you got me', and Melissa will come and help you out. Everything is expected to run smoothly, but if by an unlucky chance we are under lockdown and we need to exit the hospital or we need to enter during lockdown, there is a secret air duct on the outside that no one is aware of. Tonight, we will go pay a visit to the manager of the hospital, we will slip the influenza pill in his food or water as it is water soluble and then we will send an email to the hospital from his email stating that James Carter will be his replacement tomorrow. Does this work, Adam?" I finished.

"Well let's not be late. We have an appointment at the manager's house," Adam said, smiling.

Chapter 14

Cameron Gilbert. Position: White Hat General
December 13, 2004, 9:00pm

We waited outside the manager's house for any sign of movement inside. We needed to know if he was inside his house or not. We decided to knock on his door pretending to be workers asking him if he needs his shingles re-done.

"Scan his house for security systems," I told Ryan.

"Good idea, Cameron," he told me and took off his backpack. He took out the scanner, which was disguised as a strut finder and pressed the scan button. Immediately the results started coming in. He had a security system with the latest motion sensors. He also had a few surveillance cameras that were armed.

"I can't tell if they have auxiliary power or not, Daniel?" Ryan said.

"I don't think these cameras have the space for a battery, but just in case, shoot it as soon as you open the door with a tranquilizer," Daniel suggested.

"I'll do it. I'll attach a scope to my rifle." James said.

"Wait. We don't need to shoot it, it will become too obvious if we shoot it, the guy will know that there was someone inside his house, we have to disguise it somehow. I say we use a mini EMP to destroy the internals of the security system and that won't alert the authorities either, it can look like a power shortage as well". I pointed out.

"Okay, here is the plan. Cameron, you will help me break in and pull all of it off. Daniel, go to the side of the house, open the window with a crowbar, then wait for instructions. James go with Daniel, aim straight for the motherboard with the mini EMP that's in the bag. Melissa, you will come in through the front door with me and Cameron, you will have to put the pill in his food. Chloe, you can take watch as well as disable his power. Are we all ready?" Ryan finished.

"YES." came a muffled reply from everyone. I took out the lock- picking set and gave it to Ryan.

"You should do it," he told me and thrust it back into my hands. I opened it up and took out the lock pick and the hair pin. I put the hair pin inside and moved it around until I heard a click, then I inserted the lock pick and turned the pick like a key.

"Okay we're clear, the door's unlocked. Chloe, how far are we on the disabling of the alarm?" Ryan asked.

"Alarm's clear, don't worry about the cameras, I put those in a loop from twenty-five minutes ago," Chloe tells us.

"Okay, that's good. Dan, crowbar on three. James, use the EMP then fill your magazine with an influenza fluid, keep watch with Chloe. Let's go on 3. 1, 2, 3." On

Ryan's word everyone moved, the door opened, I heard the window open and we all ran in. Melissa went straight for the kitchen while we went to find the managers laptop. He had it on his couch and it was an Apple iBook G4.

"Not the easiest thing to hack, but it'll work," I told Cameron. We opened it up and it went straight to the Apple loading screen and then to the users. We clicked Joseph Patterson's user and it went to password, we inserted a USB and it bypassed the password and we were in. We opened his browser and logged on to his email and sent an email to his secretary saying that he will be unable to come to the office tomorrow because he is sick.

"Okay, Cameron, hack into his email when we get back to HQ. We need to be able to see everything on his email before him; he should only be able to see what we want him to see; all emails he sends must go through us. Okay everyone, let's go," Ryan finished and closed the laptop and removed the USB. We exited through the window, everyone but Ryan, who was locking the door and then the window. He re-armed the security system and left through the window. We all waited for him outside. "There is a black van parked on the other side of the street, the one we came in. I'll call it. Thankfully this one has a real driver." Ryan pushed a button on his belt and a black van zoomed in from behind the curb. "Okay, let's go," Ryan said and opened the back door of the van and hopped in. We all pile in and we see Ryan sitting at the computer working on a case.

"What are you doing?" Chloe asked him.

"Writing my log," he answered. He then turned around and looked at us as the van started moving, "Melissa, did you put the pill in his food"? he asked.

"Yes," she answered.

"Chloe, do we have a daily schedule for him?" Ryan asked.

"Yes, he leaves his house for a walk without eating, and then comes back in 30 minutes. Based on the time we took today, he is coming home in around five minutes," she answered.

"Okay, let's get back to base see what Adam thinks," Ryan answered and we remained silent for the rest of the ride.

Once we got back to base Adam greets us impatiently, "You took way too long, what if he had come back in the middle!"

"We did what we could," Ryan answered.

"NO, RYAN, YOU CAN NOT JUST GO AROUND LIKE THAT TAKING YOUR TIME. ANONYMOUS IS NOT TAKING THEIR TIME," Adam yelled.

"Look, Adam, just calm do–"

"No, Ryan, he has no right to yell at us, he makes us do all the work, sitting on his fat ass all day and then yells at us for taking 30 seconds extra," James cut in.

"James, shut up, Adam is working harder than anyone–"

James interjected before Melissa could finish, "Oh, don't give me that shit" The beeping starts in the background "I've been ruining relationships being here, but my boss here doesn't care about anyone but himself and Melissa Taylor, who he is watching out for the most – the rest is Ryan's responsibility. I can't keep up with this anymore, I quit," James finished and stomped out.

"I'll talk to him," Ryan said and walked away.

"Well I'll get going," Daniel said and walked away.

"Me too," Chloe said.

"I'll go too," I said and walked away, leaving Melissa and Adam alone in the corridor.

Chapter 15

James Miller. Position: White Hat Colonel
December 14, 2004, 6:00am

When Ryan came after me, I had never thought that he would be able to convince me to return. His persuasiveness surprised me. He told me that Adam was very stressed because he thought this was all his fault. He told me how Adam's best friend, then his cousin, joined Anonymous and how much pressure must be on him since he needed everything to be done right. So, I told him that I would turn up tomorrow at six o'clock in the morning and here I am. He asked everyone to come to the base at 6:00 am. So here I was, in the almost empty base, surrounded by thirteen new members and waiting for a familiar face. Then I saw Daniel, Ryan and Cameron walking into the base.

"Hi James, feeling any better?" Cameron asked.

"No way, I might not look like the guy for emotions, but half of my friends have left for California to become stars in Hollywood, and Katie has been cheating on me," I told them.

"So, should we call this Young Adult Drama or what, since Teen Drama doesn't exactly work for this scenario?" Daniel asked.

"It's 6 am, why are we here so early anyway?" I asked Ryan.

"Because we need to arrive before the hospital opens, and at least you got some sleep. I've been here all night," Ryan replied.

"You big fat liar, I saw you leave right after talking to me," I retorted.

"Well then, James, I hope there is some brain in that over-inflated skull of yours, because I got a call fifteen minutes later that the manager had gotten an email and the night shift had no idea what to do. In fact, they had no idea what to do the entire night, so I had to stay here all night. Adam didn't even turn up and they said he and Melissa weren't picking up since their phones had been turned off," Ryan finished.

"I think it is happening," I told them.

"Please refrain from being the gossip queen in this headquarters," came Adam's voice from behind us. We turned around and saw him and Melissa standing behind us. "By the way Ryan, thanks for covering last night, I was uhh, busy. You will be getting a promotion," Adam told Ryan.

"For my amazing detective work or for working last night?" Ryan asks.

"What do you mean?" Adam asked.

"Your dinner was at a fine dining steakhouse, where you told Melissa you liked her; she agreed to go out with you. You spent three hours eating, then talked during the car ride home. During that ride, Melissa made you give your phone to her so that you don't stay up all night, and you arrived together since she needed to give you back your phone, and since your mom went back to Cincinnati, no one was there to question you who as to who Melissa is. What do you think?" Ryan finished. Honestly, I was amazed that Ryan was able to deduce such things all by himself.

"How did you do this?" Adam asked Ryan.

"It is simple mathematics based on what James exposed last night and…"

"Cut the shit, Ryan, I know you didn't do math to figure this out," Melissa cut in.

"Okay, okay, Adam left his earpiece on," Ryan told them.

"Well, that is fair enough," Cameron said.

"What is the range on these things, the nearest steak house is 30 miles away" Chloe says surprised.

"Wait if Ryan made a program to stop swearing in HQ, then why does it only happen when I swear"? I asked.

"The program was designed for you, not for anyone else. Daniel answered.

"Anyways, Ryan, I am promoting you to Lieutenant General of The Good Hackers," Adam said. "If everyone works as hard as him, you will all be getting promoted. Oh, look, Chloe is here," Adam said, pointing at the door. "Good, everyone load into the van, you will all be briefed by Ryan in there," Adam finished.

Ryan started walking towards the garage, so we all followed him; then he stopped and turned to us. "Grab whatever you are assigned from the armory, I will load up the van." We all started moving into the armory. I grabbed a night gun pistol and a tactical knife. I saw Ryan grabbing three snipers and rifles as well. I walked into the van where I saw five other members sitting down. I climbed into the van with Melissa and Chloe behind me. Cameron and Daniel were helping Ryan. Thirty seconds later Ryan, Daniel, and Cameron climbed into the van, their arms laden with weapons that we could use. "So, these snipers will be positioned in vans around the hospital. They were the best in combat and in shooting during training and Adam has agreed to let me use them for today. So, let's go break into a hospital."

Chapter 16

Daniel Wang. Position: White Hat General
December 14, 2004, 7:15am

I did not notice when the truck pulled to a stop, a block from the hospital. I was deep in thought about something that had once been said by the great Arnold Palmer, "You must play boldly to win." Were we playing boldly? Were we going to win if we exposed ourselves every single day? That brought me to my next point: "What is not done today is never finished tomorrow," said by Johann Wolfgang von Goethe. If we waited, not exposing ourselves every day, not risking our lives every day, then we would never win. This proves that first we must win the battle within ourselves, and believe me, there is a huge one going on inside me. When I saw everyone getting out, I followed in pursuit and walked over to Ryan, who was talking to the driver of the van. "So, take the snipers to their designated spots. I'll be in the van control center. There is another car waiting on the next street. Walk there and go back to base and come back in four hours; we'll need a driver. If you are late, I will start driving," Ryan finished telling the driver. He nodded and

Ryan got in the back of the van. "Keep in mind that I will come to your aid if ever you need me. Cameron, or should I say James, you will be going in first, telling the secretary that you are James Carter and will be led to your office. Three minutes after that, Christian Brown will enter the building and the secretary will call you down to sign the documents to let him in. Then Allison Gray will enter the building and will go to the front desk, show her pass, and take a seat at an empty desk. Daniel will enter and will need to go through with identification. Therefore, he will provide his badge to the secretary, who is Chloe, and she will approve his entry. Melissa will enter as a guest, visiting patient Liam Jones. This is how this is going down, any questions?" Ryan finished.

"Umm, how come Daniel and Melissa don't have an alias?" James asked.

"They don't need one. Melissa will not have to sign in or anything, and Daniel will be ID'd by Chloe, so no problem there. If anyone asks you Melissa, your name is Anneka and Daniel, you can be Nick." Ryan answered. We all spread out as Cameron entered first.

"So I've just entered the hospital, I see the secretary's desk ahead. Hi, my name is James Carter, I am the temporary Case Manager." We all listened as the secretary typed on her keyboard. "Okay, I am just going to need some ID from you to prove that you are James Carter and then I will have someone lead you to your office. So, your responsibilities are simple, just make sure that everything is running smoothly, if you run into any problem with the staff then you are being given permission to fire them," we heard the secretary say over the earpiece. "Okay guys, she has approved me, Christian, you're up," Cameron said. From a distance we see James walk into the hospital and we heard him slap his false driver's license onto the secretary's counter.

"Christian Brown, new Head of Human Resources," James said, sounding bored.

"Okay, I'll just call down the Case Manager to approve your joining." We heard her pick up the intercom, "paging James Carter to the front desk, James Carter to the front desk, thank you. Now we just have to wait for Mr Carter and then you can go to your new office," the secretary finished. We heard Cameron approach, greet James, sign a few papers, and walk away. We then heard James being led to his office. Later Chloe entered the building, and presented her pass, and took her seat behind the desk. Then I walked through the door, and said, "Medical assistant," as I gave my pass to Chloe. She scanned it and gave it back to me saying, "Thank you very much," and I walked away towards the locker rooms where I scanned my pass again and entered.

"Okay Ryan, I'm in, what's next?" I said into my earpiece.

"Wait for Melissa to go in, then you will have to go through the escort of Darren," Ryan replied. I saw Melissa walk in through the glass in the locker rooms and she went and told Chloe that she is here to see patient Liam Jones. Then she walked towards the entrance to the mental health ward. "Would secretaries Abigail, Alexis and Annika please come to the Human Resources office, thank you," we all heard James say over the PA system.

"Guys, we have a problem, there is still one secretary at the desk," Chloe said over the earpiece, "and there's more, she is Amy Simpson."

Chapter 17

Cameron Gilbert. Position: White Hat General
December 14, 2004, 8:30am

We had never expected Anonymous to be at the hospital today, we had never even expected Anonymous to know that Darren was in this hospital. "Okay, let's take this slowly. Daniel, I need you to scour the hospital in search of more Anonymous members. Melissa, take aim at Amy Simpson from a distance and Chloe, get her as close as you can to an open window. I'll disable the recording on the CCTV systems," Ryan said into his earpiece. Since I had not been named among this group, I went onto the manager's computer, and I changed up the electronic file with an SD card which contained the file. When I was done, I decided that I can be of some use to The Good Hackers, so I turned on the security feed and looked at what was going on downstairs in the main lobby. I could see Amy Simpson with a gun to Chloe's back as Amy opened the window. It looked like she was planning to throw Chloe out of the window and make it look like suicide or an accident.

"Ryan, tell the sniper to shoot at window three, floor one; he'll see a figure at the window and over her shoulder is someone who needs to be shot," I said into my earpiece.

"Copy that, Cameron, have you switched on the electronic file yet?" Ryan asked.

"Yeah, I got it done before I looked at the security feed," I answered.

"Okay, good, I passed the message on to the sniper. He's preparing a steady shot. Daniel, did you find anything?" Ryan asks.

"All of the original Anonymous members are here, with a few others. Give me the word and I'll take action," Daniel said.

"No," Ryan replied, "Cameron, you go on the employee list and figure out how many of the Anonymous members are here today. To blend in they will have to be doing their jobs," Ryan said. I checked the list of employees, and to my surprise found that ten were currently at the hospital, and more than half of them working as volunteers.

"Ryan, I am going to take care of those people, has the sniper fired yet?" I asked.

"Yes, Amy Simpson is down, we had Chloe open the window and throw her out of the building," Ryan replied. "As for taking people out, you can do that discreetly and make sure that all CCTV recordings are disabled. You can also find reason to fire maximum two of the Anonymous employees for not being at their workstation, etc. Good luck," Ryan said.

"Guys, we are going on to code silver, we need a lockdown, now, now, now," Chloe said. "They are commencing the transport of Darren. Melissa and Daniel, hurry over to ward 3213; he was found there, trying to jump out the window. They were taking him to his ward, and then he was to be sent to the mental hospital. If we want to make sure that Darren doesn't fall back into Anonymous's hands, then we better stay alert," Chloe finished. I stood up, printed out a list of the Anonymous members who were currently disguised in the hospital, and headed out, closing the door behind me. Number one was Janet Ross, an employee of Human Resources. That meant that James was in immediate danger.

"James, Janet Ross is currently working for you as a Human Resources employee. You might want to take her out," I told James. I headed towards the cafeteria as the other Anonymous member, Mia Brown, was placed there. I walked into the cafeteria and headed towards the McDonalds which had a short line. There I saw Mia Brown, taking the order of the current person at the front of the line.

"Hello Mia, I would like to speak with you about your work here," I told her. She told someone to cover for her, then followed me to my office. "So, Mia, do you know who I am?" I asked her.

"The Case Manager," she answered.

"No, I am the person who is about to shoot you," I said as I drew my gun and pointed it at her.

"No matter how hard you try, you will never be able to bring down Anonymous," she yelled back.

"Tell me Mia, what drives you to work for these people, when there is a chance that you can stop them?" I asked her.

"White hat hacking is no fun, at most, all you see is some idiots trying to hack Apple and failing badly. Jackson was helping out a friend and no matter how much anyone tries to deny it, Adam is the reason Anonymous exists. There is no point in trying to save the world when you can wreak havoc, have the entire world at your feet, begging for mercy," she rebuked.

"That's deep," I tell her, "goodbye." She reached for her back pocket, but before she could do that, I shot her with a tranquilizer dart.

"Ryan, tell Adam that Mia is down. We have gone into lockdown; the only way for lockdown to end is if I say so. I also think that today is a ruse and that they don't actually want Darren back. Looking at the list the only non-beginner Anonymous members here are Janet and Amy out of ten. Darren has been transported, his ward has been locked down, I am restarting the CCTV, and we are getting out of here. James, you can quit now."

"Right! On it," James said. And about five minutes later I got a call saying that we will have to recruit a new Head of Human Resources and that one of the employees of Human Resources had just vanished. I was also told that one of our patients was being immediately transferred to a mental hospital and I needed to come down to sign the transfer forms. I walked into the elevator and hit the button labeled (FLOOR 1). When I got down there, I saw Darren subdued by a straitjacket and two nurses who were holding him. I signed the forms and loaded him into the ambulance myself to supervise the transfer so that it went smoothly (not intercepted by Anonymous). During the ride all we discussed through our ear pieces was how to keep him from getting into the hands of Jackson. After around 30 minutes we arrived at the mental hospital. I talked with the manager there, completed the patient transfer, making sure to let the administrator know that this patient shouldn't be allowed visitors or have an accessible profile, and then I left. When we got back to the hospital, I called it a day and told the head secretary to handle everything if anything comes up. I told Ryan I was coming to the van but noticed there were two. I opened one and saw how much I missed in an hour. The Good Hackers rounded up eight people, tranquilized them, and threw them into the truck. I slammed the door and climbed into the other truck. I saw everyone sitting in the truck, with blank faces.

"What happened?" I asked.

"Anonymous stole all the assets and money from the Bank of America. They literally emptied the accounts. They have taken credit for this already." Ryan finished.

Chapter 18

Melissa Taylor. Position: White Hat General
December 14, 2004, 1:45pm

Everyone's mood was at a breaking point. We had been silent the whole ride but when we got back to the base, we saw everyone chattering and Adam came running to us.

"We may have failed earlier, but this is our chance to recover. Anonymous has taken control of the radios of air traffic control and is threatening a plane crash," Adam told us excitedly. We all rushed out of the van, while Ryan explained the second van to Adam. We hurried over towards our desks, and sat down, while one of the televisions was turned to the news channel which was broadcasting the status of this situation live.

We watched as Ryan came and sat down at his desk. "Do we know which aircrafts are being threatened to crash?"

"They are Boeing 737s," Maria told him.

"Okay, let's try to hack into the aircraft's radio," I instructed Katie Garcia. "We'll be able to communicate with the pilots." I sat down at my desk attempting every code I could think of to hack into the transmissions.

"Why don't we just intercept the transmissions instead of hacking them?" Daniel says.

"I've got live feed," Cameron shouts.

"Okay, now turn up the speaker's volume to 100%," Ryan said.

"This is Delta flight 4535. We are off course; is there anything we need to be made aware of?" we heard.

"Delta flight 4535, this is air traffic control. We have had to make a few new arrangements as you were on a collision course with another aircraft. You are now completely safe; we will direct you to a separate runway." We recognized Jackson's voice.

"Is it possible for us to alert the pilots, without alerting Anonymous?" James asked.

"Doesn't look like it, … wait, we could access the PA system, but it is highly probable that we will scare the passengers," Adam said while thinking.

"There may already be some panic if some of the passengers are watching Live News. I know some of the airlines recently introduced Live Air systems via satellites." Ryan said it while thinking. "Okay, we'll work on accessing their PA System," Ryan told Adam and went and sat down at his desk.

"Sir, we have got access!" Katie yells. "Going live in three, two, one," Ryan said. "Hello, we are The Good Hackers. There is a high chance that you have not heard of us, because we have remained in secrecy for some time. We do not want to stay in the spotlight. If any of you are currently watching the news, then you would know that your pilots are being guided to a crash. We did not want to alert the organization behind this hijack, that's why we were contacting you; therefore, we decided to use the PA system. We will be putting you through to the real air traffic control. As for the organization behind this hijack, they are known as the Anonymous Hackers. You may not have known but this is not their first crime. Earlier today they stole hundreds of millions of dollars from the Bank of America. You must be warned; they lurk amongst you. They will not stop until they have terrorized every one of you. They are the electronic terrorists. This is the reason that we came to be. We are a large operation, we will try our best to stop every one of their attacks but we are not always there. We will not always be able to stop Anonymous; therefore, we need your help. We need the outside world to remain vigilant, as from now on you all are aware of the threats that Anonymous pose to our society. We will now reconnect your pilots to air traffic control." Ryan stopped talking and flicked a switch to end the announcement. "Okay, Katie, I need you to do this, login to our systems, use code gc35782, scroll until you see the icon for traffic dash air, right click it and click open as admin and do not confuse it with traffic dash plane. Now you will see the list for the control towers around Ohio. Now in the code bar, enter the code 614. Once that is entered click on COLUMBUS OHIO AIR TRAFFIC CONTROL TOWER 3479. You will then see the icons for the outgoing and incoming transmissions. Open them both on a split screen. For outgoing, select transmission 266696687 dash uncertified. That is Anonymous, written in the telephone coordination as we learned from James. Now right click that transmission and hit the mute icon. Then right click that again and hit the remove and ban from server icon.

Then focus on all the muted outgoing transmissions. Unmute them all and reconnect the proper one to the aircraft that is off course." Ryan ended his instructions.

"It is done, sir," Katie replied.

"Ladies and gentlemen, congratulations!" Ryan said as everyone applauded our victory.

Chapter 19

Cameron Gilbert. Position: White Hat General
December 14, 2004, 3:00pm

We continued to monitor the correspondence between air traffic control and the aircraft until the aircraft was safely on the ground. Once that was over, Daniel decided to call it a day and left with Ryan. James also left but none of us were clear why. Chloe remained at command with Katie, Maria and the rest of the crew. I walked over to Adam and started talking to him about the mission. All in all, we started discussing the new crew. "So, the new crew has had a lot to do since they joined," Adam told me.

"I couldn't agree more; but looking at how everyone only knows Katie and Maria's names, it might take a while for all of them to have something to do. We all only know their names and therefore when we need something done quickly, we ask them. Eventually they will break under the pressure," I told Adam.

"Well, I don't expect the team to memorize everyone's name, but I will speak to them," Adam responded.

"Well, I guess I'll get going. Let me know if you need me," I told him and started to walk away.

"Wait, since it was delayed today and yesterday, we will commence the planning for Operation Downfall tomorrow," Adam called out to me.

...

December 15, 2004, 4:30 pm

When I arrived at HQ, I was summoned to the meeting room, where I saw that everyone except James was present. I took my seat at the table. "So welcome to this meeting, we can see that James is running a bit late, so we will start without him and fill him in on the key points later on. First off, we feel we may have an informant on the inside, as every time we tried to commence Operation Downfall, we hit a road block. Also, there is no record of who sent Darren to the hospital, and someone also informed Anonymous that Darren was at the hospital. I have turned off all the cameras in this room, so no one is able to see what we discuss. This room is sound proof thanks to Ryan and Daniel, so we need not worry about being overheard. In the matter of op–" Adam was cut off by the television which had suddenly come on.

"Hello, we are Anonymous, but you already knew that, didn't you, Ryan Hall, Chloe Bennet, Daniel Wang, Cameron Gilbert, Melissa Taylor and of course, Adam Brown? You may be wondering why we didn't mention James Miller. He is currently in our custody, being beaten for what he has done to work against our organization as will all of you. You will all face the wrath of Anonymous. You may have won a couple of times, but we have also achieved victory and soon will beat you completely, and yes, we are always one step ahead of you. We will get our revenge as well as ruin you and your government." A man, in a vendetta mask, with a voice changer was mocking us. "You may try to stop us in any way, expose our members, but what is coming is much bigger. Much, much bigger, and this time you won't be there to stop it," and he raised a gun and shot straight at the camera and the screen blacked out.

Well, we needed to get James out of this mess, but before we could do that, I had to tell the team some news. "I was actually going to tell you guys this yesterday but in all the havoc, I forgot about it completely. My uncle, a millionaire, bought me a super yacht as a birthday gift a few months back. I had it converted into a carrier for The Good Hackers, just letting you know that it's a perfect place to lay a trap for Anonymous. But right now, let's focus on getting James back. Here's what I suggest. Let's set up a meet between The Good Hackers and Anonymous to discuss their demands. During that meet you guys could break in to the Anonymous base and get James back. Meanwhile, we should also focus on Operation Downfall and exposing the Anonymous operation and all those involved. I feel we should start with setting up a meet on the carrier with Anonymous, no weapons or anything, but set up tranquilizer darts in the cameras so that we can take out the majors. We also need Jackson to be there."

"Chloe, set up a meet with Anonymous on the carrier. Ryan, try to work to track down James. It is our top priority," Adam ordered as we all left the meeting room.

"Adam, I know how to contact Anonymous, should I contact them?" Chloe asked.

"Yes, go ahead," Adam answered. Chloe picked up the phone and dialed a number. She connected the phone to the speakers.

"Hello Good Hackers, it's about time you called, when and where should we set up the meet? The where will be decided by you, the when, by us. So where?"

"I'm thinking at the carrier that we own around Grim Creek," Chloe answered.

"Okay, tomorrow, five thirty pm. Adam Brown, Ryan Hall, Cameron Gilbert and Daniel Wang all have to be present. Don't be late," the person said.

"Rodriguez also must be present," Chloe says.

"He will. James will not be coming. If the meet is successful, we will send him to you, or else he will face certain death. Until tomorrow, Good Hackers." The call ended.

"We will arrange for both Cameron and Daniel to be put into protection. They must not be present tomorrow," Ryan said to Adam as I thought about what he was saying.

"You mustn't either, Ryan," Adam replied.

"No, I will be there, you cannot stop me," Ryan replied.

"I should be there, too," I told Ryan.

"Don't you understand, Cameron, they are assembling a hit team to take us out, why do you think they told us specifically to be there?" Ryan told me.

"They won't negotiate if we are absent, though," Daniel told him.

"We have two reasons we are going there. Number one is to delay so you can get into the Anonymous base to get James. Number two so we can take Jackson out." This was becoming a suicide mission for everyone who would be present at the meet. "The carrier will be empty apart from us so no one else gets hurt. The negotiating is just a ruse. We know we probably won't make it out. At least you guys should go ahead and live your lives," Ryan finished.

"That is complete nonsense! We are a team; therefore, we should do things together, not let one of us die. If we all go together, then maybe we'll have a better chance at defeating Anonymous. And anyways, I won't let you go, even if I have to shoot you," Melissa said as she reached for her gun, but she was too slow. With a small pop, Melissa fell to the ground. At first, I didn't know what happened, but then I saw Ryan lowering his pistol and I realized that he had shot her with a tranquilizer before she made any rash decision.

"Is there anyone else who wants to go against us?" Ryan asked. No one stepped forward.

"Okay then, let's enjoy the little time we have left in this world and decide how we will get James back," Adam said.

Chapter 20

Ryan Hall. Position: White Hat General
December 15, 2004, 5:15pm

This is my last log; it will not be complete. We all know that. I will hide it and it will be retrieved by The Good Hackers a bit after the meet is over. I want to let The Good Hackers know that I have been very happy with the work they have been doing these days. I am very proud of my team specifically. We can succeed with our mission only if we do not count our losses and focus on our victories and how to get more. If we get Jackson today, Anonymous will be disbanded. Jackson is too arrogant to appoint anyone to succeed him, he thinks that we do not know what he is doing. I am disappointed to say that we must fall into his plan to implement our own. Let Melissa know that I am deeply sorry for shooting her. Hopefully someday she will find it in her heart to forgive me. I know how Adam feels about this as well. He could have lived a normal life but he decided to pursue the destruction of black hat hacking. One day his dreams will be realized. If there is one thing I can ask of anyone who reads this, it is that they do not do anything stupid. Do not try to take Anonymous out on their own. They will be disbanded but will continue, not as an organization but as a group of people who seem to have regular lives but hide the truth in plain sight. I would like to thank The Good Hackers for all their hard work. I am currently standing outside the carrier. I am ready to die.

This is Ryan Hall, signing out.

...

Cameron Gilbert Position: White Hat General

December 15, 2004, 5:15pm

We were in our positions outside the Anonymous base. Waiting for Ryan to confirm Jackson's arrival at the carrier. "Okay, guys, Jackson's team has arrived. He is there with them. It's been great knowing you," and he closed his ear piece. We can still hear what's going on in Adam's earpiece.

"Good evening, Jackson, I can't say it's particularly good to see you. However, we need a deal."

"I agree. You seem to have many resources, considering the fact that you have a pile of shit at home," Jackson answered.

"Am I just supposed to be a third wheel in this or what? Let's go inside," we heard Ryan say. We hear muffled footsteps and the opening of a door.

"Okay, since Ryan isn't here, I'm going to stay and keep in contact with Adam. I'll also see what's happening in the carrier. Chloe, take the Alpha team to the rendezvous point, wait for the all clear from the Bravo, and blow up the front entrance with a C-4. Daniel, take Charlie and the Delta team and with their help, take out security. Get into the main command center and steal every plan for an upcoming attack. Then Delta can go get

James out. Once he's out, we bomb the place and move out. I don't want anyone to be smart. Ryan and Adam are risking their lives for this. Make sure no one gets hurt. Get them all out before throwing in the C-4s. Now go, go, go." Cameron tells us.

We were about to commence the operation and saw James come running out. His brown hair was full of blood and his face was badly bruised.

"It's a trap, make sure no one goes in, they have abandoned the base, it's got motion- triggered bombs. All the data in there is useless if we all die getting it," James shouts at us.

"How did you escape without triggering them?" I ask.

"I escaped before they armed them. I was just getting some information. apparently the boat's track has been calculated and a torpedo will hit it sometime around 6 pm. I don't know how they plan on saving Jackson but that's not what we should focus on; it's how we will save Adam and Ryan. We should tell them to ditch now. Is there any way you guys can take out the Anonymous team?" James asked.

"Yes, the cameras are integrated with tranquilizer darts," Daniel answers.

"What is it with you and tranquilizer darts?" James asked, irritated. "Okay, never mind that, can you access them remotely?" James asked, waving away his previous question.

"Yes, but the aiming system for the tranquilizers is separate from the camera, so we have to aim the tranquilizer gun separately using another camera and same for the other," Chloe said.

"Okay, number one, I did not understand a single thing that you just said! Number two, how are we supposed to use another camera to aim a tranquilizer gun that's mounted beside the camera?" James asked, puzzled.

"The technology we have isn't advanced enough to mount the tranquilizer directly onto the camera," Chloe answered him.

"Well then, what the hell does 'integrated' mean?" James yelled impatiently.

"That was an accident on Daniel's part, but can we please get on with saving Adam and Ryan?" I tried to calm them.

"Fine, let's get to it," James answered.

Chapter 21

Chloe Chapman. Position: White Hat Brigadier General
December 15, 2004, 5:55pm

"Careful now," I said as I directed James through the last gun aiming. He was constantly getting frustrated, so the rest of us tried to keep him calm.

"Okay, they are all set. Now if you tell me there is a timer and then it will shoot, I will burn this place to the ground with all of you in it," James promised, annoyed.

"Number one, that's not saying much since this is a van; number two, there is no timer. You have to click a button and they all will shoot," Cameron replied.

"What if we miss?" I asked.

"Then the operation fails, and we have put Ryan and Adam in danger," Daniel answered. Then the telephone rang.

"Hello," I answer. "Hello, this is Tony from HQ, uhhh, Melissa left the base," Tony says.

"Okay, we'll do something about it," I told him and ended the call. "So there has been a minor development, Melissa escaped," I informed everyone.

"May I ask what the shit you mean by escaped, was she a double agent?" James inquired.

"No, she is trying to end this operation herself. Ryan shot her, so I don't think she's very happy with him," Daniel answered.

"Well, Melissa won't be able to get to Ryan and Adam while they are on the carrier. How come Jackson hasn't brought up the absence of Cameron and Daniel?" I asked.

"We don't know, but the current demands are ten million dollars in bearer bonds, and ten million in untraceable bills. The funny thing is that they have currently not told us what they will do for us," Cameron shared the information with us. He gave us all a set of headphones and we listened in on what was happening.

"...how are we supposed to get that kind of money?" Adam asked.

"We don't care how you get it, only that you have twenty-four hours to do so or else Miller is gone," Rodriguez answered.

"Adam, James is with us, they abandoned the base and it's filled with bombs. They have no leverage without James," Cameron spoke into his earpiece.

"I will not agree to that, since James escaped and is currently with our team. You have no leverage whatsoever, do you?" Adam said.

"You have had contact with your team, you have broken the rules of our agreement. It doesn't work like this; now we will have to finish you. Goodbye," Jackson said.

"SHOOT! SHOOT! SHOOT!" James yelled and hit the button. The two members of Anonymous with Jackson fell to the ground; as they stood up, one of the bullets missed Jackson. Ryan stood up and rammed Jackson against a wall and punched him repeatedly. Jackson managed to grab Ryan's hand and put it behind his back and broke it, then slammed his head on the table. Adam stood up and attacked Jackson, being able to push him away from Ryan, but Jackson managed to knee him in the stomach. Winded, Ryan reached for a flower pot and started swinging it at Jackson, but Jackson was able to grab the flower pot from his hand and broke it on Adam's head. Ryan stood up and started to fight Jackson, and I never noticed that Cameron had gotten into the front seat of the car and was driving us to Alum Creek Lake.

"James, grab a rifle, we are almost there, what's happening on the live feed?" Cameron yelled.

"Adam's on the floor but he's trying to get up, and Jackson just broke the window with Ryan's head," I answered him. "Those windows were polycarbonate, that's two hundred times stronger than glass. I don't think even he could survive that," Cameron said.

"He's a black belt, but he's not fighting back, he's delaying so that the ship burns with Jackson on it," James told us.

"We're here," Cameron says. We got out and saw Melissa running towards the lake as well.

"You just ran six miles!" James said in astonishment.

"STFU, James, where are they?" Melissa asked.

“At sea, the exact location is unknown, Ryan’s almost dead, Adam is still fighting back,” James answered.

“As I said before, shut up, James. Is this true, Daniel?” Melissa asked.

“Yes,” Daniel answered sadly.

“There is a speedboat right there, let’s take it,” Cameron pointed out. As we all boarded the boat, we had no idea what was going to happen.

Chapter 22

Daniel Wang. Position: White Hat General
December 15, 2004, 7:35pm

We were on the carrier; most of it was a blur. We decided that some of us would keep watch on the deck while the rest of us would go ahead and look for Adam and Ryan. Cameron, Melissa and I went to find Adam and Ryan. They are currently in the interrogation room, so we raced to the second floor and to the interrogation room. We opened the door and, "Jackson Rodriguez, step away from Adam Brown and Ryan Hall," Melissa ordered.

"Melissa Taylor, as you might have noticed you are too late," he said putting his hands up and walking towards the door.

"Adam, can you get up?" Melissa asked as she helped him up.

"R-Ryan," Adam said.

"We'll send someone to get him once you're down in the boat," she said. We walked towards the exit but halfway there Jackson stopped.

"As I said before, you're too late." He took a red detonator out of his pocket and pressed down. I braced for what might be the end of my life. But nothing happened on my end. I heard the noise on the other side of the room. I had only one thought. Ryan. Cameron and I charged towards the other side of the carrier, not knowing, not caring what would happen next. When we got to the room, we were met by a blazing fire. No one could have survived that, not even Ryan. I fell to my knees. I had no words to voice my disappointment, in myself. This was my fault. I was responsible for this. Those were the thoughts going through my head. Cameron put his hand on my shoulder; there was nothing we could do for him. Suddenly, the whole carrier shook as if an earthquake had happened, but I knew it wasn't an earthquake. The torpedo had struck the carrier. I could feel the ship teetering to the side barrelling towards land. We ran back to Melissa, Adam and Jackson. He was laughing. I had no words to express the hate I was feeling.

"I think we should go check if Chloe and James are okay," I said, my voice cracking. I ran up the stairs to see Chloe lying on the floor.

"What happened to her?" I asked James.

"She hit her head on a pole while walking. Honestly, I don't even know why she's still out cold, what happened with you?" he asked.

"Ryan's dead," I answered coldly.

"Huh." He was shocked. "Well, we're barreling towards land, so I'd tell the people downstairs to brace for impact because I give us two minutes tops."

I ran downstairs and go talk to Melissa. “Chloe’s out cold, and we’re speeding towards land. James said brace for impact,” I told her.

“Okay,” she answered. Adam sat down against a wall and put his head between his arms. Filled with dread Melissa grabbed a railing, still pointing her gun at Jackson, and Cameron and I went to sit on the benches, not knowing what was going to happen, or if I would make it out. A few minutes later we felt the impact and saw the side of the ship collapse. Melissa’s gun fell from her hand, Cameron and I went flying across the room and Jackson also fell to the floor. Smoke began filling up the cabin. Then we saw Jackson stand up, gun in hand and starting to speak, “You’ve had it good for too long, Adam, you’ve cherished your success, but enough, you know yourself that Anonymous will continue with or without me, but The Good Hackers need you or Ryan, but he’s dead, so I guess for you, it’s lights out.” We heard the gun shot. As smoke filled up the room, we all fell unconscious.

Chapter 23

Adam Brown. Position: To be determined
December 20, 2004, 00:45am

I sat in my room holding my head in my hands, tears in my eyes. I was overcome by the feelings of anger and deep sorrow in my heart and too many thoughts in my mind: I shouldn't have fought with Jackson in the first place. I could have simply ignored his hacking into the university, I shouldn't have initiated The Good Hackers, I shouldn't have involved anyone else and kept it to myself, but then how could I have possibly stopped him alone? I should have informed the authorities but no point of informing as they could not have done anything.

One part of me wanted to go kill every single member of Anonymous, but I knew this is not me; I have never believed in violence. I also knew that Ryan would never allow any violence either and I have to respect his ideology. Besides, we stood up against Anonymous to do what is just; we cannot become the unjust. I knew that Anonymous won the fight, but should I let them win the battle by turning into one of them?

I lost my good friend; we as The Good Hackers lost a very good friend and the most reliable member of our team. “I can’t let his life just go like that,” I talked to myself again and again.

Once again, I started going through all the logs and I went through them again and again and again becoming hysterical trying to learn what we did wrong. Where did we make a mistake? What could have been done differently which could have changed the final result? I guess I was still not out of the shock at losing Ryan, my very good friend.

December 22, 2004, 11:30pm – Present Time

I am walking in a dark alley; I can hear wolves howling from afar in response to the howl off in the distance. This walk feels like the longest walk I have ever had. This alley ends at a warehouse. I am standing at the door, thinking about five years back when I took the first lesson of hacking from my guru. Whatever I know about hacking today is because of him.

I am not sure whether he would like to help me. He may decide not to see me at all. He may simply say no to any proposition. But I have to give it a try because if anyone, and I mean anyone, can help me stop Anonymous, it’s him. I didn’t come this far to go back without him helping me. I have to give it a try, but then what do I have to offer him? Why would he risk his life for me? It will be a risk to anyone’s life who decides to become part of stopping Anonymous. My hand goes up to knock at the door and then goes down without knocking. This action repeats three times, but I am not able to gather the courage to knock at the door for help.

Suddenly, I hear the sound of the door unlocking and a heavy voice emerges, "Come on in, Adam, I have been expecting you. I am with you in taking Anonymous down." I hear Ash's voice, my guru's voice. I can never forget his voice. His affirmation without me even saying what I have come here for makes him true to his name, one in a million. His acceptance has given me hope and a sense of happiness for the first time in so many days.

www.ingramcontent.com/pod-product-compliance
Ingram Content Group UK Ltd.
Pitfield, Milton Keynes, MK11 3LW, UK
UKHW041845200726
13854UKWH00005BA/2184

9 781788 306843